Down the Street

Written by Andrea Butler

Illustrations by Bo Sterk

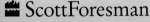
ScottForesman

A Division of HarperCollins*Publishers*

Bells on my toes.
Bells on my toes.

Jingle-jangle, jingle-jangle.
Bells on my toes.

Shakers in my hands.
Shakers in my hands.

Chickee-che, chickee-che.
Shakers in my hands.

5

Drum on my chest.
Drum on my chest.

Bang, bang, bang, bang.
Drum on my chest.

Dance down the street.
Dance down the street.
Cha-cha-cha, cha-cha-cha.
Dance down the street.